Usborne Publishing Limited proudly presents:

MYSTERY ON MAIN STREET

Written by
Tony Allan

Based on a story by
Tony Allan (What, him again?), Rachael Robinson, Mark Fowler
& Phil Roxbee Cox (That can't be his real name.)

Illustrated by
Ann Johns

Designed by
Paul Greenleaf & Ann Johns (Didn't she do the pictures?)

Puzzles by
Mark Fowler and Tim Preston

Hand lettering by
Rachel Bladon

Edited by Rachael Robinson (That kept her busy!)

Assisted by Michelle Bates

Directed by Gaby Waters

Hypnoman Comic Strip

Written by
Phil Roxbee Cox

Designed and illustrated by
Andy Dixon (Hey, he can do two things at once.)

Lettering by
Gordon Robson

With special thanks to the mayor and citizens of Mainsville
and the makers of Disguise-O-Matic, without whose help this
story would not have been possible.

Contents

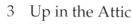

3	Up in the Attic	22	Evil Intentions
8	The Crystal's Message	24	Juke Joint Jitters
10	Materializing on Main Street	26	At the Junkyard
		28	Creature Feature
12	Guessing Games	30	Nightmare on Main Street
14	Hair-raising Escapades	32	The Old Dark House
16	The Drop Before the Hop	34	The Big Parade
		36	Floating
18	Meet the Motorvators	38	Rats in a Trap
20	Trouble on Wheels	40	Saving the Stone
		42	Back with a Bump

About this book

Mystery on Main Street is a thrilling adventure story, packed with fiendish codes and puzzles which must be solved to unravel the plot. Most of the puzzles are pretty difficult, so don't be surprised if you get stuck. There are clues on page 43 and you will find all the answers at the back of the book. If you don't need to look at these, you may well be a genius.

Up in the Attic

Exploring the attic in his Uncle Jack's farmhouse one rainy afternoon, Tim came across a box of comic books. They were old ones saved from when his uncle was a boy. Intrigued, Tim leafed through them and one in particular caught his eye. It was about a superhero he had never heard of before. He read on . . .

NOORT DNANO ORDUO YGNIE
IN THE SOLAR SYSTEM OF GLUMM, ALL IS NOT WELL ON THE PLANET OH-NO...
THERE'S LITTLE TIME LEFT. THE HYPNOSTONE MUSTN'T BE ALLOWED TO FALL INTO THE HANDS OF THE NAMTAR...
...WITH IT, HE COULD RULE THE UNIVERSE!
I HAVE USED THE SACRED LAZER OF OUCH TO SPLIT THE STONE INTO TWO HALVES. THESE MUST BE SENT AS FAR AWAY FROM EACH OTHER AS POSSIBLE!
YOU, TROON, MUST TAKE ONE HALF TO THE PLANET EARTH, WHILE YOU, DROON, MUST TAKE THE OTHER HALF TO SYPHON IV!
PRINCES TROON AND DROON HURRY TO THEIR SEPARATE SPACE CRAFTS...
TO EARTH!
TO SYPHON IV!
GOOD LUCK, MY SONS. THE FATE OF THE ENTIRE UNIVERSE RESTS IN YOUR HANDS!
...BUT MOMENTS AFTER THE CRAFTS HAVE LEFT, THE NAMTAR'S MEN— LED BY THE EVIL MINION— BURST INTO THE LAUNCH PAD...
SEIZE THEM!!
ESOTD RAWRO FKOOL
SKNAH TYNAM
YOU'RE TOO LATE, MINION! YOUR MASTER WILL NEVER FIND THE HYPNOSTONE NOW!
A FIGURE STEPS OUT OF THE SHADOWS...
I WOULDN'T BE SO SURE, FOUR EYES... TAKE HIM AWAY!
SOMETIME LATER, ON EARTH...
ISN'T THIS GREAT? I WISH THE VACATION WOULD NEVER END!
TONIGHT'S OUR LAST NIGHT UNDER THE STARS!
WHERE'S BRAD?
STILL LOOKING FOR BUGS!
YOU'RE A BEAUT!
BUT MILD-MANNERED ENTOMOLOGIST * BRAD BRADLEY IS ABOUT TO MEET A SPECIMEN HE DIDN'T BARGAIN FOR...
GASP! WHO ARE YOU?!
* THAT MEANS "A BUG-LOVER", FOLKS. —EDITOR!
EGASS EMEHT REHPI

Tim groaned. The rest of the page was missing! Frantically, he searched through the box of comic books … and then the whole attic … but he couldn't find it anywhere.

He sighed and picked up the comic book again, trying to guess what happened next in the story. He was gripped. Flipping through the pages, something caught his eye. There were groups of letters dotted around the white frames of some of the pictures. It looked like a kind of coded message.

What does the comic book message say?

The Crystal's Message

Tim sat wondering about the "badge" that was referred to in the message. Just then, he heard his Aunt Polly's voice calling him down for supper. Tim tried asking about the comic books, between bites of bread, but his uncle only chuckled and said that he hadn't looked at them in years. Then Tim asked him about "Hypnoman".

The farmer looked puzzled. "I don't remember him," he said.

Tim tried to jog his uncle's memory by mentioning Troon and Droon and the evil Namtar, but Uncle Jack simply shrugged. "What else did you find up there?" he asked.

Tim mentioned an old wind-up gramophone and some family photo albums, but his mind was on the strange message he had deciphered. He couldn't wait to return to the attic.

As soon as he could, Tim hurried back up the ladder into the roof. He hauled himself through the hatch and there, right in front of him, was the missing page. Why hadn't he spotted it before?

Tim quickly scanned the pictures, and noticed something strange. The half of the Hypnostone that Hypnoman wore as a badge was covered in symbols. Tim realized it must be another message!

What do the mysterious symbols mean?

Materializing on Main Street

Without thinking, Tim said the decoded message out loud. The moment the words left his lips, he felt himself being jolted into the air by some invisible force.

He sensed he was being swept higher and higher. He began spinning faster and faster, and a terrible giddiness came over him . . . then everything went blank.

When he came to, he still felt dizzy. He shook his head and rubbed his eyes. He found himself by a busy street, only it didn't look like any street he'd ever been on before. The cars were bigger for starters. Then his eyes caught on something that startled him even more.

A ghostly shape was materializing in front of him. The figure looked strangely familiar. The cloak . . . the face.

"Hypnoman?" Tim said weakly, rubbing the back of his head. "But you're not real."

"Says who, kid?" the ghostly figure sighed. "The fact is, I need your help."

"*My* help?" Tim stammered. "How can *I* help *you*?"

"Right now I'm only the shadow of my superhero self," said the comic book figure, and Tim couldn't argue with that.

"There's not much I can do on my own. At least, not until I can get back into three dimensions. That's where you come in." Hypnoman continued, "I need my half of the Hypnostone to get back into action. But now it's gone, and I reckon the Namtar must have it. You've got to help me get it back. Otherwise . . ." He paused and a look of pain crossed his face. "Otherwise, the Earth could fall into the hands of this evil swine."

Tim gulped. "That still doesn't explain what I can do to help," he said.

I can't stay materialized for long.

"We've got one thing to work on – the boardgame I found in the street. The one who dropped it was the one who got me with the gas. I'd recognize him again, mask or no mask. It could be a clue. You'll find it in my hotel room. Just tell them you're Brad Bradley."

Before Hypnoman had a chance to say which hotel, he faded away to nothing. What should Tim do? This was hopeless. Suddenly a smile crossed his face. "I know where to go," he cried.

Which hotel should he go to?

11

Guessing Games

Tim set off through Mainsville in search of the hotel. Everything was strange: the hairstyles, the girls' long dresses, and the huge cars. It all looked to him like something from a film or . . . well, comic book. He could tell from the looks he got from other people that he seemed just as odd to them.

He located the hotel without much trouble and got the key to Brad Bradley's room. Searching through Hypnoman's belongings, he found the boardgame lying under some clothes at the bottom of a drawer.

Tim lifted the lid off the box. Some of the names on the board seemed strangely familiar. Then he realized that he was looking at a map of Mainsville disguised to look like a game! There were rules and a list of moves too. He guessed at once that they must contain directions, but where to?

Where do the directions lead?

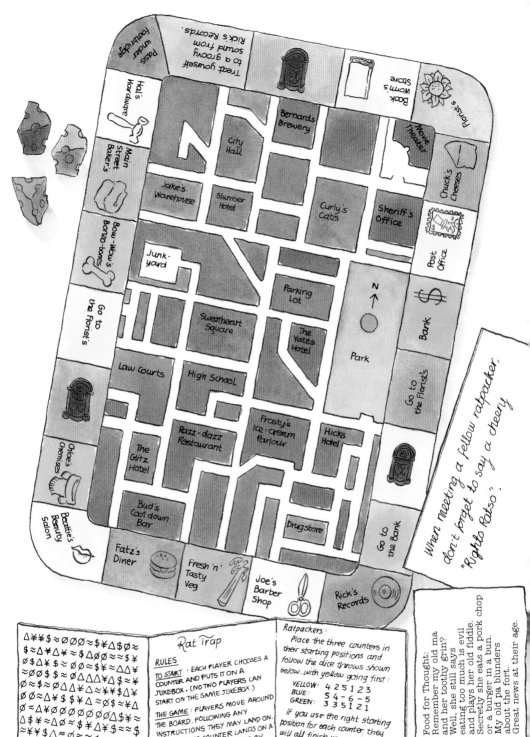

Rat Trap

RULES

TO START : EACH PLAYER CHOOSES A COUNTER AND PUTS IT ON A JUKEBOX. (NO TWO PLAYERS CAN START ON THE SAME JUKEBOX.)

THE GAME : PLAYERS MOVE AROUND THE BOARD, FOLLOWING ANY INSTRUCTIONS THEY MAY LAND ON. IF A PLAYER'S COUNTER LANDS ON A SQUARE ALREADY OCCUPIED BY ANOTHER COUNTER, HE/SHE MUST MISS A TURN.

Ratpackers :
Place the three counters in their starting positions and follow the dice throws shown below, with yellow going first:

YELLOW: 4 2 5 1 2 3
BLUE: 5 4 - 6 - 5
GREEN: 3 3 5 1 2 1

If you use the right starting position for each counter they will all finish up on the same square after six turns. Go here for further instructions.

Food for Thought:
Remember my old ma
and her toothy grin?
Well, she still says
eating too much is evil
and plays her old fiddle.
Secretly she eats a pork chop
or a burger in a bun.
My old pa blunders
about the fort.
Great news at their age.

When meeting a fellow ratpacker, don't forget to say a cheery "Rights Ratso".

13

Hair-raising Escapades

Before setting off for the barber shop, Tim tried on one of Brad Bradley's shirts and a pair of jeans. They were a good fit. He studied himself in the mirror. He looked more like a "local" now. In his new disguise he felt better equipped to face whatever lay ahead.

Main Street was busy at that time of day. People were ordering hot dogs and playing with children in the park. Tim shuddered at the thought of the Namtar and the threat of intergalactic evil hanging over the whole town . . . the whole *universe*.

The barbershop was in the south-east corner of town. The place was packed with barbers, but nobody else. All the chairs were empty. Six pairs of eyes watched Tim expectantly. Studying their reflection, he recognized one of the men from somewhere.

Tim knew it was one of the Namtar's followers, but couldn't think where he had seen him before. Tim sat down in the man's chair and muttered "Right Ratso". He expected some kind of a reaction from him, but there was none.

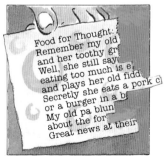

Food for Thought:
Remember my old
and her toothy gr
Well, she still say
eating too much is e
and plays her old fidd
Secretly she eats a pork c
or a burger in a b
My old pa blun
about the for
Great news at their

What he got was a haircut. Tim stared in horror at his reflection. He looked like his father did in old photos! Tim was beginning to think that he'd picked the wrong man until something was slipped into his hand.

It was a torn card, and Tim knew that he had seen one like it before. Perhaps it was a kind of message.

Which barber works for the Namtar, and can you find the hidden message?

The Drop Before the Hop

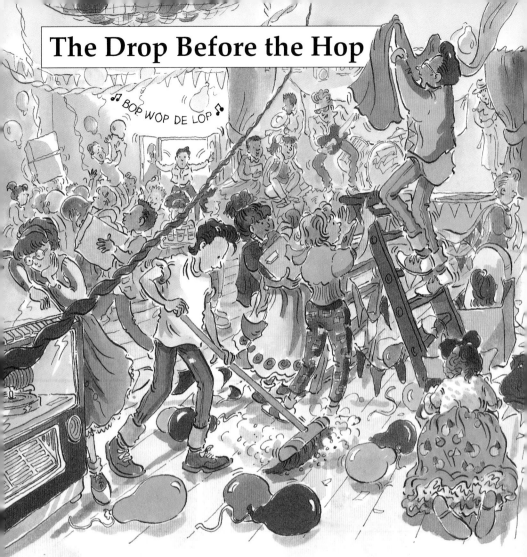

♪ BOP WOP DE LOP ♪

The note referred to the "Mainsville Hop" and, according to a poster Tim had seen, the only hop was at the high school. This was where he went next. He found the place in chaos. Everyone was helping get the hall ready for the big dance which was the school's contribution to the town centenary celebrations.

Boys were perched on ladders hanging up streamers. Girls in bobby socks were blowing up balloons.

A band was rehearsing at the front of a stage, and people were shouting. No one seemed to mind the noise because everyone was too busy getting ready to have a good time.

Tim forced his way through the crowd to the stage. He could see a trapdoor at the back that looked as if it opened onto storage space below. That was where he had to go. Quick as a flash, he lifted the trap and ducked inside.

It was dark under the stage, and there wasn't much headroom. Tim almost had to bend double. He edged along gingerly, wishing he still had the oil lamp he'd used in the attic.

He took one more step and found himself treading on thin air. He was falling, turning head over heels as he dropped. Landing with a bump, he lay still for a second, hoping nothing was broken. Then, looking around in the gloom, he found a bag. Inside was what looked like a map, and some pieces of paper. One had some sort of message scrawled on it. This had to be what he was looking for. But what did it all mean?

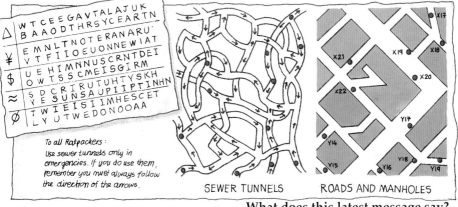

```
  W T C E E G A V T A L A J U K
△ B A A O D T H R S Y C E A R T N
  E M N L T N O T E R A N A R U
¥ V T F I I O E U O N N E W I A T
  U E H I M N N U S C R N T D E I
$ O W T S S C M E I S G I R M
  S D C R T R U T U H T Y S K H
≈ Y E S U N S A U P I I P T I N H N
  T W I E I S I I M H E S C E T
∅ L Y U T W E D O N O O A A
```

To all Ratpackers:
Use sewer tunnels only in emergencies. If you do use them, remember you must always follow the direction of the arrows.

SEWER TUNNELS   ROADS AND MANHOLES

What does this latest message say?

Meet the Motorvators

Tim was wondering who this "Ratman" was who had sent the coded instructions, when he heard a voice call out to him. Fighting back his fear, Tim stuck his head through the trap. Eight pairs of eyes stared down at him.

"Are you sure that's him?" asked a leather clad figure, frowning. Another one nodded and pointed. "Look, he's wearing the transmogrifier on his wrist!" Their faces broke into smiles.

It dawned on Tim that watches like his were unknown in Mainsville . . .

. . . and these people seemed to like it. A girl who seemed to be in charge slapped him on the shoulder.

"My name's Sal, and I'm leader of the Mainsville Motorvators," she said. "We've been looking for you and I'll tell you why . . ."

"What happened next?" Tim asked.

"As he slipped, we grabbed this guy's hand," said Sal. "In the confusion, we got away with his glove, and a message he was clutching in it. The only trouble is, we can't figure out what it means."

What does the message say?

Trouble on Wheels

The Motorvators were impressed with Tim's decoding skills. "That's the second message I've seen from Ratman," he said, as they walked out onto the street. "He must be working for an evil outer space genius called the Namtar. Unless, of course …"

"This is no time for talking. Jump on," Sal shouted.

Step on the gas.

Eight engines roared to life. "To the junkyard!" Sal commanded. The Motorvators were ready for action. Tim hung on for dear life as the bikes shot off down the street.

"How come you got mixed up in this?" Sal called over her shoulder. Tim was about to answer when a battered green truck shot past, blaring its horn.

STEAL -A- TRUCK

"Roadhogs!" Sal shouted. The bike veered as she pointed a finger at the passenger in the truck.

"Hey. I know that woman!" she yelled. "She was the one at Mainsville Milk-Bar. After her!"

Sal and Tim took off after the truck, leaving the rest of the Motorvators to head for the junkyard.

The truck rounded a corner and skidded to a halt. The woman leaped out. Before Sal and Tim could catch her, she jumped onto a passing bus moments before the door closed. Sal screeched to a halt and parked the bike.

Frantically, she waved down a cab. "Follow that bus!" Sal yelled at the startled driver. "The woman will be expecting us to keep following her on the bike," she explained to Tim. "She won't be suspicious of a cab."

"I hope you've got some money to pay for the ride," said Tim.

The cab swung around a corner just in time for them to see the woman get off the bus and scuttle down an alleyway.

Tim and Sal jumped from the cab and ran after her. Turning a corner, they found that the woman had vanished. "She can't just have disappeared," gasped Sal.

Tim pointed at a manhole cover. "She must have gone down there," he said."Trust one of Ratman's ratpackers to use the sewer system."

"We'll never catch her now," sighed Sal, feeling defeated.

"I think I'll be able to tell you exactly where this ratpacker is heading," he beamed triumphantly.

"You don't have X-Ray eyes do you?" Sal asked. After all, Tim was a superhero's sidekick.

"No," Tim laughed. "But I do have a good memory. This ratpacker may even lead us to Ratman himself. Let's go back and fetch your bike. We may arrive before her."

Where is the ratpacker heading?

Evil Intentions

It was midday when Tim and Sal arrived at Bernard's Brewery. One of the huge wooden doors was slightly ajar. Was Ratman inside?

"After you," said Sal. "After all, it was your map that got us here." They slipped inside what turned out to be one enormous room. Empty beer barrels littered the cold stone floor.

There was no sign of the woman or any other ratpackers. Tim found a photograph of her among other items strewn across a table top. Sal's eyes widened and she pointed to the words "Sonic Boom Bomb" printed across the top of a piece of paper. "We've got to stop them," she cried.

Where has the Sonic Boom Bomb been planted?

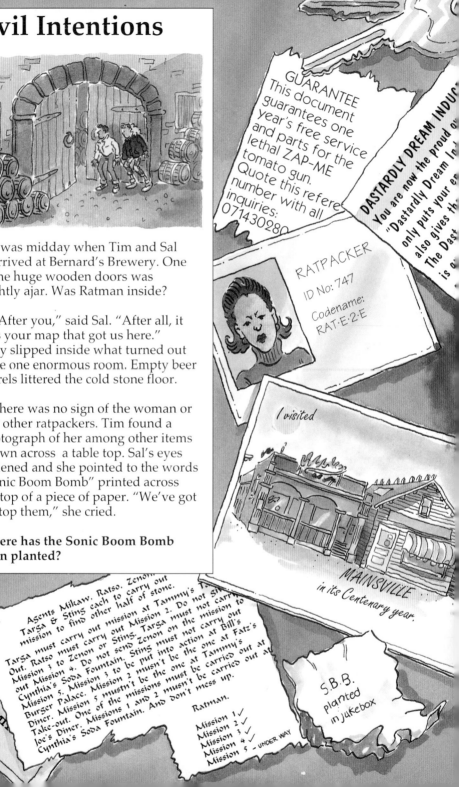

GUARANTEE
This document guarantees one year's free service and parts for the lethal ZAP-ME tomato gun. Quote this refere number with all inquiries: 071430280

DASTARDLY DREAM INDUC
You are now the proud o
"Dastardly Dream Ind
only puts your en
also gives the
The Das
is a

RATPACKER
ID No: 747
Codename:
RAT·E·2·E

I visited

MAINSVILLE
in its Centenary year.

Agents Mikaw, Ratso, Zenon
Targa & Sting each to carry out
mission to find other half of stone.
Targa must carry out mission at Tammy's
Out. Ratso must carry out Mission 2. Do not s
Mission 3 to Zenon or Sting. Targa must not carr
out Mission 4. Do not send Zenon on the mission to
Cynthia's Soda Fountain. Sting must not carry out
Mission 5. Mission 3 to be put into action at Bill's
Burger Palace. Mission 2 musn't be the one at Fatz's
Diner. Mission 5 musn't be the one at Tammy's
Take-out. One of the missions must be carried out at
Joe's Diner. Missions 1 and 2 musn't be carried out at
Cynthia's Soda Fountain. And don't mess up.

Ratman.

Mission 1 ✓
Mission 2 ✓
Mission 3 ✓
Mission 4 ✓
Mission 5 – UNDER WAY

S.B.B.
planted
in jukebox

Movie theater

ADMI

WANTED · WANTED · WANTED ·

This boy is known to be working for HYPNOMAN. He answers to the name of Tim.

He is dangerous and wears this strange device on his wrist.

To: The Namtar
From: Minion, your most faithful follower.

Dear Great and Powerful One

I have discovered that here in Mainsville there are many different groups of motorbikers. These bikers are a great threat to our mission. Members of some of these gangs wear special signs on their helmets or jackets. These are the signs we know about:

The Beavers ◎ The Tomcats ✻
The Wrinklies ≋ The Towts ◼
The Makaws ◆ The Tombstones ◢

In addition, we have gathered the following information:
Members of the Beavers ride blue bikes.
The Wrinklies' bikes do not have orange or blue stickers.
The Makaws do not ride red bikes.
The Tombstones's bikes do not have white stickers.
The Towts do not ride bikes with pink or orange stickers.
The most dangerous of these gangs is the Motorvators, but members of this gang cannot be easily identified. I hope this information is useful.

Monster: AAARRRGGGHHH!

David: If only I could distract it for long enough for Professor Jones to reach the lab.

Place D.D.I.
Susan: Don't be a fool, David. It could crush you underfoot like some insignificant little insect.

David: It's the future of this great big beautiful world of ours we have to think about now, honey, not my own worthless skin.

Press 'activate' button
Susan: Worthless? The mistakes you made were a long time ago, darling. You're a good man. You've so much to give . . .

LEAVE!
Monster: AAARRRGGGHHH!

Susan: David! Wait . . . Come back . . .

Fellow Vermin.
Those four-eyed-do-gooders Troon and Droon have sent out an intergalactic plea for help in the guise of an Earthling's comic book.
The ratpacker who finds and destroys this pathetic plea for help shall be heaped with praises, and avoid my wrath.

Ratman

P.S Find me that other half of the stone.

MISSION 5
Planting **Sonic Boom B**
in jukebox

This bomb will give off an earsplitting scream, a nasty headaches for up to twelve hours. Once the p have fled, search for the other half of the stone.

The Sound, Fire, Power and Disarm buttons must each be wired up to one of four buttons on the jukebox. Use only one button in each row. Use only one button in each column. The Sound button should be seven numbers greater than the Fire button. The Power button must be five numbers less than the Disarm button. The Fire button must not be in the top row. The Power button must not be in the left hand column.
All praise to Ratman.

23

Juke Joint Jitters

They had to get to Fatz's Diner, and fast. Sal somehow managed to squeeze even more speed out of the bike. Tim clung on as she weaved a path through the traffic. The diner lay right on the other side of town.

When they arrived, they found the parking lot thick with huge vehicles. The place was obviously popular with truckers. Sal skidded to a halt by the front door, and the two went dashing into the diner.

"We've got to get everyone out of here," said Sal pushing her way through the crowd. "The Sonic Boom Bomb could boom at any moment."

"There isn't time," Tim shouted above the noise of the jukebox. "We're going to have to try to deactivate the sonic bomb ourselves."

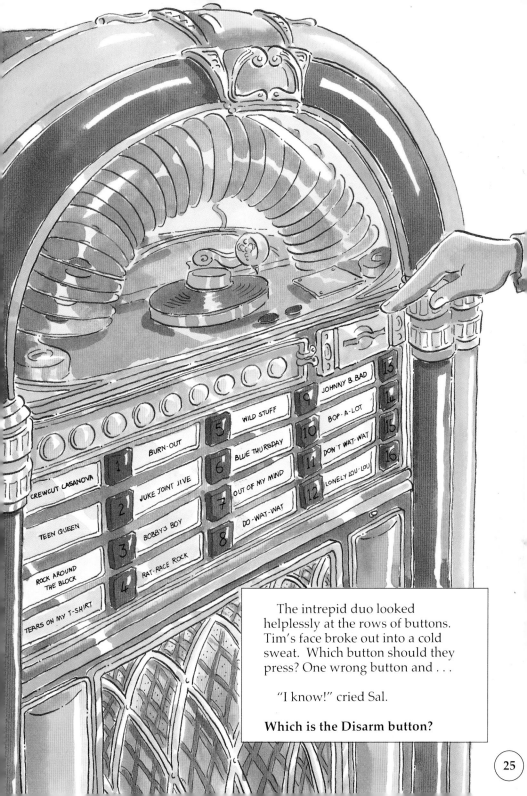

The intrepid duo looked helplessly at the rows of buttons. Tim's face broke out into a cold sweat. Which button should they press? One wrong button and . . .

"I know!" cried Sal.

Which is the Disarm button?

(Labels on the jukebox buttons:)

CREWCUT CASANOVA
TEEN QUEEN
ROCK AROUND THE BLOCK
TEARS ON MY T-SHIRT

1 BURN-OUT
2 JUKE JOINT JIVE
3 BOBBY'S BOY
4 RAT-RACE ROCK

5 WILD STUFF
6 BLUE THURSDAY
7 OUT OF MY MIND
8 DO-WAT-WAT

9 JOHNNY B. BAD
10 BOP-A-LOT
11 DON'T WAT-WAT
12 LONELY LOU-LOU

13
14
15
16

At the Junkyard

As Tim and Sal left the diner, Ace, a Motorvator, rode up in a cloud of dust. "Found you at last!" she gasped. "Ratman's gang caught two of us at the junkyard. We need help." They sped off to the scene of the action, swerving to avoid roadblocks that were being erected in the streets.

They picked themselves up in time to see the truck speeding out of the gates. Hypnoman faded away before their eyes, his good deed done.

"We'll never catch those ratpackers," Sal groaned.

"Yes, we will," cried Ace. "I know where they're going. And that," she said, pointing to a poster on a wall, "will help us to avoid the roadblocks."

Where are they going, and by what route?

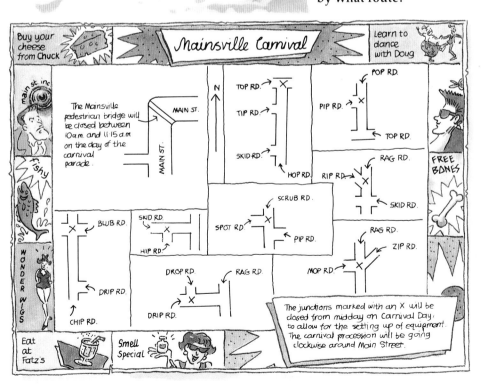

Buy your cheese from Chuck

Mainsville Carnival

Learn to dance with Doug

main st. inc

The Mainsville pedestrian bridge will be closed between 10 a.m. and 11.15 a.m. on the day of the carnival parade.

N

MAIN ST.

MAIN ST.

TOP RD.

TIP RD.

SKID RD.

HOP RD.

PIP RD.

POP RD.

TOP RD.

RIP RD.

RAG RD.

SKID RD.

fishy

SCRUB RD.

SPOT RD.

PIP RD.

RAG RD.

ZIP RD.

FREE BONES

SKID RD.

BLUB RD.

HIP RD.

DROP RD.

RAG RD.

MOP RD.

W O N D E R W I G S

DRIP RD.

CHIP RD.

DRIP RD.

The junctions marked with an X will be closed from midday on Carnival Day, to allow for the setting up of equipment. The carnival procession will be going clockwise around Main Street.

Eat at Fatz's

Smell Special

27

Creature Feature

Starring Nash Randall + Nanci Sparkle

Mainsville Movie Theater was full when Tim, Sal and Ace arrived. The main feature was already halfway through. It was a monster movie in 3-D, and everyone was wearing special glasses.

Tim and Sal were standing uncertainly in the aisle wondering what to do next when a voice boomed from the screen.

That sounds familiar, Tim thought. Then he remembered where he'd come across the words before. He had to do something, and fast.

What is about to happen?

Nightmare on Main Street

Tim scanned the seats anxiously. Suddenly a man stood up and headed for the exit. Tim was about to follow him when he noticed that the man had left something behind.

Tim ran up to his seat. A red light was winking, and wreaths of gas were starting to drift from a funnel on the top. It must be a Dastardly Dream Inducer!

Quick everyone, clear the building. You haven't got much time.

There's a Dastardly Dream Inducer in here and it's about to pump out sleeping gas.

It'll give you the worst nightmares you've ever had!

There was a stampede as frantic movie-goers fled the auditorium, tearing off their 3-D glasses as they ran. Some had already been affected by the fiendish device.

Tim and Sal pushed their way through the crowd of moaning people, trying to catch sight of the rat packer who had planted the dream inducer and fled.

"There he is," cried Ace, running up to them. She pointed to the man leaping onto a moped. "It's no good following him on my bike. It's covered in a cloud of sleeping gas."

A grateful stranger threw Tim the keys to his machine. There were six motorbikes in the pile he had pointed to, and six bike owners standing around it.

Which bike should they take?

The Old Dark House

The engine roared to life, and Sal and Ace took off with Tim hanging on for dear life behind them. "Wooah!" he moaned.

Halfway down Main Street they caught sight of the ratpacker. "Don't lose him!" Sal shouted. "He's the only lead we've got."

The moped screeched to a halt. They watched its rider pull himself over a fence.

They slunk after him, taking care not to let him know that he was being followed.

On the outskirts of town, they reached an old house. The man walked purposefully inside.

Tim made his way up to the house and peered through the window. There was no one around. Warily he pushed open the front door. The hall was empty, and he couldn't hear a sound. He beckoned to the others and they went in.

It was Tim who found the missing Motorvators bound and gagged in the basement. Mick, the taller of the two bikers, managed to hand him a piece of paper. Tim ripped off the gags.

"There was an argument between our kidnappers," said Mick, between gulps of fresh air. "One of them was refusing to take written orders from Ratman . . . until this arrived."

Tim studied the message that the kidnappers had left behind. It looked a cross between a poem and a secret code. His face broke into a grin. Suddenly, the riddle made sense to him.

What does the riddle mean?

CAN YOU NOT SEE WHO I REALLY AM?
THEN HOLD A MIRROR TO THIS PAGE.
THAT WAY YOU'LL UNDERSTAND MY SCAM
AND AVOID THE OUTCOME OF MY RAGE.
TIME IS RUNNING OUT, YOU KNOW:
THIS POWERFUL CRYSTAL MUST BE FOUND.
TO THE NEXT LOCATION YOU MUST GO,
AND SEARCH THE PLACE WITHOUT A SOUND.
FIND THE STAR, THEN TRAVEL THREE,
THERE AT ONCE YOU'LL FIND THE START.
NOW TRAVEL TWO TOWARDS THE SUN,
THEN THREE, THEN TWO, THEN FOUR THEN ONE.
ALWAYS GO ALONG THE LINES, BUT TURNING CORNERS IS ALLOWED.
NOW TAKE THE LAST OF MY TRUE NAME,
AND THEN THE FOURTH, MY LOYAL FRIENDS.
AT LAST YOUR TASK IS CLEAR. FAIL NOT –
FOR HE WHO FAILS IN CHAINS SHALL ROT. ЯATMAN
P.S. (if you land on a symbol, it's a real pain : go back to the start and try again!)

The Big Parade

Tim whistled. Ratman wasn't *working* for the Namtar . . . He *was* the Namtar. Tim wondered how many other names and identities this intergalactic arch-villain might have.

"Sounds to me like we're gonna need help," said Sal. "We can start by trying the Sheriff."

Back in town, the note on the Sheriff's office door said it all. Now what should they do?

Main Street was blocked solid. They gazed at the seething mass of people. "The Namtar-Ratman is probably out there somewhere," groaned Sal. "And we don't even know what he looks like."

Tim's eyes sparkled. "But if he's on a float, I think I know which one it is!"

Which float belongs to the Namtar-Ratman?

Floating

Tim pointed out the Namtar-Ratman's float to Sal. In a flash, she sprinted over to the other Motorvators lined up by the roadside watching the procession. She shouted something to them . . .

. . . then swung back into the road toward the Namtar's float, waving to Tim to follow her. The next thing he knew they were under the moving float, hanging perilously close to the road surface below.

"Go right to the front!" Sal called, inching her way forward.

"What's the idea?" Tim cried, his eyes wide in terror. One slip, and he could be crushed under the wheels.

"When we reach the footbridge, pull that lever to disconnect the float from the driver's cab," Sal hissed.

How do they know when they've reached the footbridge?

Ooops!

32

Rats in a Trap

As the float came away from the driver's cab, Tim and Sal jumped clear before the front of the float crashed to the ground. Unaware of what was happening behind him, the driver of the float's cab carried on driving. Chaos reigned. The stranded float was hit by another which, in turn, was hit by another . . . Spectators scattered as the drivers behind stamped on their brakes, sending their vehicles skidding.

Amidst the chaos, Tim noticed a familiar, ghostly figure just visible on the sidewalk. Hypnoman looked sheepish. "Er . . . sorry," the superhero muttered. "I'm a little late to help." Then, brightening up, he added, "But I guess you guys managed fine on your own."

. . . am I too late to help?

Tim was still trying to guess what the rest of Sal's plan could be, when he caught sight of the other Motorvators. They were lined up on top of the footbridge. In their hands was something that looked familiar. Of course, the net that had held the balloons at the high school hop!

At a word of command from Sal, the net came down on the stranded float. The bikers had surprise on their side. The ratpackers were caught like rats in a trap. The more they struggled to free themselves, the more the villainous vermin became ensnared.

"Got you at last – " Tim started to shout, but the words stuck in his throat.

He had seen someone and something that made him freeze on the spot. It was obvious that their problems weren't over yet.

What two things has Tim spotted?

Saving the Stone

Tim launched himself at the Namtar, knocking the tomato gun from his hand and sending it flying. As the villain flailed helplessly in the meshes, something fell from his pocket, glinting in the sunlight. It was Hypnoman's half of the Hypnostone. Triumphantly, Tim snatched it up.

What do you kids think you're doing?

"One half to go," he muttered. "Then the universe'll be safe again." Just then a police car screeched to a halt in front of the stranded float. The Sheriff climbed out of it.

"These people are arch-villains," Tim said proudly. He handed Hypnoman the crystal.

With my half of the stone back, I feel better already.

His superhero powers restored, Hypnoman set off after the driver's cab. He returned, holding a familiar figure by the scruff of his neck.

What a day!

Here's the driver of the float, Sheriff. Another one for you to lock up.

Drats! Why don't things ever go right for me?

As the Namtar's ratpackers were led away by the Sheriff, Hypnoman pointed to the sky. Tim and Sal saw a gleaming, saucer-shaped object shoot across the blue.

Whereabouts in Mainsville did you hide your half of the stone, Droon?

That's my secret, Troon. The main thing is that we have it back now.

The revitalized superhero pointed after the vessel. "Droon and Troon," he said proudly. "Our cosmic comrades. They must have found what they were looking for. We needn't worry about the other half of the Hypnostone any more. It's in safe hands."

Meanwhile a terrible change had come over one of the Sheriff's prisoners.

Half man. Half rat. All vermin. I'll be back.

All I said was "The power is in the stone".

Rats. Here I go again!

The Sheriff stepped back in disbelief. "Would someone mind telling me just exactly what's going on?" he wailed.

Tim did his best to explain. "It all started with the message on Hypnoman's half of the Hypnostone," he said. And then he repeated the mysterious words . . .

41

Back with a Bump

Tim blinked. He was back in his uncle's attic. Come to think of it, had he ever really left it? He sat up, rubbing his eyes. . .

. . . and caught sight of himself in an old mirror.

Then he found a single frame from the comic book. Tim smiled.

The character standing next to the fully restored superhero looked very familiar.

Clues

Pages 6-7
If you look through the comic strip you will find a hidden message. Working from back to front could be a good way to start.

Pages 8-9
Think back to the other coded message in the comic strip.

Pages 10-11
The comic strip is the starting point. Then, just keep your eyes peeled and remember that Brad likes baths.

Pages 12-13
Once you have found the right starting position for each die, you're well on your way to solving the puzzle. There are six possible combinations to try out.

Pages 14-15
Look back in the comic strip and see if you can see a familiar face. Have you seen this card before? Strangely enough, the letters which *don't* appear may turn out to be more significant than those which do.

Pages 16-17
Where have you seen these symbols before? How can you make sense of the lists of letters using these symbols?

Pages 18-19
The zig zag pattern is the key to crack the code.

Pages 20-21
Turn back to the boardgame and look for a place name. Although the scales are different, you can use the road map, sewer map and boardgame to find the essential starting point for the one-way system of sewer tunnels.

Pages 22-23
The piece of paper labelled Mission 5 and Ratman's note for his agents will help you.

Pages 24-25
Start by working out all the possible positions for the Sound, Fire, Power, and Disarm buttons. Then try out each combination to see which one works with only one button in each column and one in each row.

Pages 26-27
Start by finding the Junction of Rag Road, Skid Road and Rip Road and the others will soon fall into place.

Pages 28-29
If you flip back a few pages the words from the 3-D movie will become even more familiar . . .

Pages 30-31
The key is to find which bike belongs to the Towt gang. It should be easy to match the bikes to their owners from there.

Pages 32-33
The name at the bottom looks doubly familiar. The riddle is obviously an instruction as to how to find some words among the symbols. Remember if you land on a symbol, you must have gone wrong somewhere.

Pages 34-35
Read the banners and flags on the floats with care. One of the companies is somehow connected to the Namtar-Ratman. Look back to the comic strip, but don't stop there to find the answer.

Pages 36-37
A number in the picture might set you off in the right direction, but which one? You'll need some maps.

Pages 38-39
Tim has seen one of these faces before, but not in the flesh. That same person is holding a potentially lethal object ...

Answers

Pages 6-7

This message is written from back to front and the letters are grouped in fives rather than in their actual words. If you start at the end of the last whole page and work your way from bottom to top along each of the pages the following message is revealed:

SPEAK THE WORDS ON THE BADGE, TO COME TO OUR AID. IF YOU DON'T UNDERSTAND OUR LANGUAGE, THE TWENTY-SIX SYMBOLS AROUND THE PERIMETER OF THE BADGE SHOULD HELP YOU TO DECIPHER THE MESSAGE. MANY THANKS. LOOK FORWARD TO SEEING YOU. DROON AND TROON.

Pages 8-9

The symbols around the edge of the Hypnostone badge represent letters of the alphabet, starting with the symbol for the letter A after the arrow sign. The arrow is there to show the reader which direction to follow the symbols.

Using this information, decoding the message is straightforward.
It reads:

THE POWER IS IN THE STONE.

Pages 10-11

Locating Brad Bradley's hotel is a matter of deduction. There are four hotels in Mainsville: The Glitz, Slumber Hotel, Hicks Hotel and Yates Hotel. They are listed on the "Welcome to Mainsville" sign in the comic strip. It is also revealed in the comic strip that Brad is staying in The Glitz as Hypnoman (look closely at the package he is left), so that rules that one out. According to a poster on page 11, Hicks Hotel only has showers but Brad is in the bath in the comic strip. This leaves either Slumber or Yates Hotel. It can't be Slumber Hotel because it is closed for repairs. A notice says so on page 10. Brad must have checked into Yates Hotel.

Pages 12-13

Each of the counters has to start on a different jukebox, so there are six possible combinations to try out. Only one combination leaves all counters on the same square at the end. This is when yellow starts on the top jukebox, blue on the left and green on the right. The square they all end on is Joe's barbershop. This is where Tim must go.

Pages 14-15

The barber who works for the Namtar is circled here. You can see him as he appears in the comic strip, as one of the Namtar's followers.

A similar card to the one on this page appears untorn on page 13. If Tim writes down the letters that are missing from the torn card and ignores the punctuation. They spell:

Mainsville hop under stage

Food for Thought:
Remember my old ma?
and her toothy grin?
Well, she still says
eating too much is evil
and plays her old fiddle
Secretly she eats a pork chop
or a burger in a bun.
My old pa blunders
about the for____
Great news at their age.

Pages 16-17

These letters and symbols only make sense when used alongside the symbols on the boardgame instructions on page 13. When a symbol appears in the boardgame message, Tim uses the first letter in the row that appears next to that symbol, then crosses it out. The next time the same symbol appears, the next letter in the row is used, and so on, until all the letters have been used.

The message reads:

> We must widen the circle. Time is running out. I must have the crystal. Ransack the junkyard, but leave it as you found it. We do not wish to arouse suspicion. My patience is wearing thin. Ratman.

Pages 18-19

Start from the top left-hand letter of the message and read diagonally down and up from left to right until you reach the top right-hand letter of the bottom row. Then carry on from the bottom right hand letter, reading diagonally up and down from right to left until you are back at the beginning again. With punctuation added, the message reads:

> I already have one half of the Hypnostone and soon I will be in possession of the other half. Once the two halves are joined ultimate power will be mine. Those loyal to me will be well rewarded. Those who fail me will suffer my vile rage. Ratman.

Pages 20-21

The ratpacker has entered Mainsville's sewer system by going down a manhole in front of a building marked "Jake's Warehouse". Jake's Warehouse is marked on the boardgame (on page 13). The manhole can then be identified on the manhole map by matching up the shape of the roads with those on the boardgame. It is manhole number X21. X21 can be found on the sewer map by its position in relation to the other manholes. From this map, Tim has realized that the ratpacker can only go to manhole Y14, using the route shown here in red. By looking back to the boardgame map you can identifiy Y14 as being by Bernard's Brewery. This is where the ratpacker must be heading.

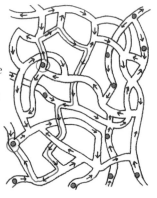

SEWER TUNNELS

Pages 22-23

By studying the three pieces of paper circled here, Sal knows that Mission 5, the planting of a Sonic Boom Bomb in a jukebox, is under way. By carefully following Ratman's instructions to his agents she can determine which mission is at which location:

Mission One: Tammy's Take Out
Mission Two: Joe's Diner
Mission Three: Bill's Burger Palace
Mission Four: Cynthia's
                 Soda Fountain
Mission Five: Fatz's Diner.

So the Sonic Boom Bomb is in the jukebox at Fatz's Diner.

Pages 24-25

Sal has remembered the instructions to Mission 5 that were on a piece of paper at Bernard's Brewery. First she and Tim note down all the possible positions for the four buttons, such that the Sound button is seven numbers greater than the Fire button, the Power button five numbers less than the Disarm button, the Fire button not in the top row and the Power button not in the left-hand column. Then they look at each possible combination of buttons and find that only one satisfies the condition of there being only one button in each row and one button in each column. They find that the Fire button is number 3, the Power button number 8, the Sound button number 10 and the button which they must press to disarm the bomb is number 13.

Pages 26-27

Ace noticed that one of the kidnapped bikers had managed to write the words "Movie Theater" in dust on the side of the truck. To find the route from the junkyard to the Movie Theater, Tim, Sal and Ace must match the junctions shown on the notice board with the roads on the boardgame to find out where all the roadblocks have been set up for the carnival. First they identify the junction of Rag Rd., Zip Rd. and Mop Rd., which is between Frosty's ice-cream parlour and Razz-dazz restaurant on the boardgame. Then, using these street names, they can find out where all the other junctions are and where the roadblocks have been set up. There is only one possible route that they can take to get to the Movie Theater avoiding the roadblocks. The route is shown here in red.

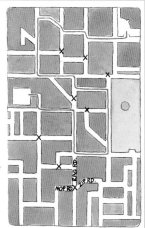

Pages 28-29

Tim hasn't heard the words from the movie before, but he has *read* them. They appear as part of a movie script in the papers they found at Bernard's Brewery on pages 22-23. Handwritten notes on the script include the letters D.D.I and the words "activate" and "leave". Another piece of paper from the brewery refers to a Dastardly Dream Inducer. Tim has realized that a ratpacker must be about to activate this fiendish device.

Pages 30-31

There are six bikes in the pile and only five of their owners standing around them (The sixth person's bike isn't in the pile). Tim and Sal must match the bikers to their bikes. To do this, they use the information Minion sent the Namtar on pages 22-23. Using this Tim and Sal work out that there is only one bike which doesn't have pink or orange stickers, so that must belong to the member of the Towt gang. This leaves only one blue bike, which must belong to the Beaver. Only one of the remaining bikes has neither orange nor blue stickers, so that must be the Wrinklies' bike. The Tombstone's bike is the only other bike without white stickers, and the Makaw's is the green one. This means that the red bike at the bottom of the pile is the only one that is ownerless and is therefore the one that they should take.

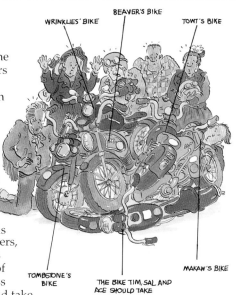

WRINKLIES' BIKE

BEAVER'S BIKE

TOWT'S BIKE

TOMBSTONE'S BIKE

THE BIKE TIM, SAL AND ACE SHOULD TAKE

MAKAW'S BIKE

Pages 32-33

If you hold **ЯATMAИ** up to a mirror, you will see the word NAMTAR. The Namtar and Ratman are the same creature. The riddle also tells the followers where to search next for the missing half of the Hypnostone. Tim follows the riddle's instructions, and finds that only one sequence of letters can be made, reading LAW COU. He then takes the last and fourth letters of Ratman's true name (the Namtar) giving him the words LAW COURT. This is where the ratpackers are supposed to go next.

Pages 34-35

Tim has spotted a float with a banner marked Main Street Inc. He remembers having seen the company name before (along with a company logo of a staring eye) in an advertizement on a noticeboard on page 27. This logo was also worn by the Namtar in the comic strip. Tim realizes that this float must belong to the intergalactic arch-villain himself!

Pages 36-37

The manhole is really the key to this clue. By comparing the manhole map to the boardgame, X20 can be located in the top northwest corner of Main Street. The noticeboard on page 27 shows that the footbridge is in that corner. This board also states that the carnival is going clockwise. Tim therefore knows that he must disconnect the float from the driver's cab when he goes over the manhole.

Pages 38-39

The "someone" Tim has recognized is the man holding the tomato. He appeared in the Main Street Inc. advertisement on the noticeboard on page 27. Tim strongly suspects that this is the Namtar-Ratman disguised in human form.

The "something" Tim has spotted is the tomato itself. He recalls having seen a guarantee for a lethal ZAP-ME tomato gun in Bernard's Brewery on page 22. It's more than likely, therefore, that this is no ordinary fruit! They are all in great danger.

First published in 1994 by Usborne Publishing Ltd, Usborne House, 83-85 Saffron Hill, London EC1N 8RT, England. Copyright © 1993 Usborne Publishing Ltd.

The name Usborne and the device 🎈 are Trade Marks of Usborne Publishing Ltd. All rights reserved.